ILLUSTRATED CLASSIC EDITIONS

King Arthur
and the Knights of the Round Table

Howard Pyle

Adapted by
Alexa Villanueva

Published by Playmore Inc., Publishers and
Waldman Publishing Corp., New York, New York

ILLUSTRATED CLASSIC EDITIONS

CONTENTS

About the Author

Howard Pyle was born in Wilmington, Delaware in 1853. After he finished high school, he went to art school. Then he worked in his father's leather shop. But Howard returned to the work he loved best, illustrating, and opened his own school especially for young artists.

He liked to create his own special worlds. He called them islands of fantasy or imagination. He would use his paint brush to capture these worlds in pictures and sometimes he wrote stories himself. There are stories of pirates, American colonial life and the legends of the days of chivalry.

In *King Arthur and the Knights of the Round Table*, we are invited into one of his favorite fantasy lands. It took seven years of researching, illustrating and writing four books on the legends of King Arthur, legends that were originally written in Old English, Welsh, French and German.

Howard gathered these tales and told them in his own way, so anyone could open a book of his at anytime, anyplace and step into his magical fantasy worlds.

Uther-Pendragon

CHAPTER 1

A Royal Birth

Many, many years ago there lived a noble king named Uther-Pendragon. He had an army of brave knights, he defeated all his enemies, and he became overlord of all England.

In his struggle against his rivals, Uther-Pendragon was aided by two great advisors. One was a powerful enchanter and prophet known afar as Merlin the Wise; the other was a renowned knight called Sir Ulfius. With the help and assistance of Merlin and Ulfius, Uther-Pendragon made peace in the kingdom he ruled with justice and compassion.

After some time, Uther-Pendragon married a beautiful, gentle queen named Igraine. Igraine was the widow of the Duke of Tintegal. Before she married Uther-Pendragon, she had already had two daughters, Margaise and Morgana le Fay.

Her daughters came with her to the court of Uther-Pendragon. The king treated them as his own daughters and arranged noble marriages for them. Yet Uther-Pendragon worried about who would be the heir to his throne.

Queen Igraine soon found out she would have a baby. Uther-Pendragon rejoiced and planned to celebrate the birth of his child. Merlin came to him in secret and warned him to tell no one about the baby.

"My lord," Merlin advised, "this must be a secret birth. When the child is born, I will tell you more."

Uther-Pendragon had learned to trust Merlin's words and his heart was painfully troubled. Queen Igraine gave birth to a beauti-

Queen Igraine with Margaise and Morgana

ful baby boy of great size and strength. The proud mother and father wrapped him in warm blankets and lay him in a royal cradle of gold and blue–the cradle of a future king.

Merlin came to the king. He was distressed with worry, his eyes sad and misty.

"My lord, you know the spirit of prophecy is strong within me. I can foresee that you shall shortly become ill with a terrible fever and will not live. Your child will be defenseless and enemies will kill or imprison him. Give me the child. Sir Ulfius and I will hide him and find a place where he can grow to manhood safe from these dangers."

"Merlin," replied Uther-Pendragon, "as far as my death is concerned - when my time comes to die, I have faith God will give me grace to meet my end with cheerfulness and strength; for, certainly all men must die whether they be kings or peasants.

"But concerning the child, if your prophecy is true, he is in great danger. Bring him to safe-

Merlin Advises His King.

ty and watch over him. For this baby is the most precious inheritance this land shall ever know."

Merlin did as he was told. During the night he and Sir Ulfius took the child away but no one knew where. Some months later, Uther-Pendragon was stricken with a sickness, as Merlin had foretold. The brave king met his death with the strength and courage he had shown throughout his life.

Once Uther-Pendragon died, it was as Merlin predicted. The kingdom fell into great mayhem. Lesser kings fought with each other to become overlord. Wicked knights and barons captured travelers and held them for ransom. Those who could not pay were killed. Injustice reigned. Knight fought knight in deadly battle, not for honor, but for gain.

People wished for a new king to bring order. The land suffered with the terrible trouble that lay upon it.

Deadly Battle

Help Us Find A Great King!

CHAPTER 2

The Search for a New King

Nearly eighteen years of great troubles passed. One day, the Archbishop of Canterbury summoned Merlin to him.

"Merlin, people say that you are the wisest man in all the world. Can you find a way to correct the problems that afflict this kingdom? Use your great knowledge to help us find a king so that we may again have happiness as we did in the days of Uther-Pendragon."

"My lord Archbishop," Merlin answered, "the spirit of prophecy shows me that this country shall soon have a king who will be even wiser and greater and more worthy of praise than Uther-Pendragon. He shall restore order and peace where there is now chaos and fighting. I may also tell you that this king shall be of Uther-Pendragon's own royal blood."

The archbishop asked Merlin how they would know the rightful king from those who only claimed to be the true king.

"My lord," answered Merlin, "I shall use my magic to create an obstacle, which, if any man shall solve it, everyone will know that man is the rightful king and leader of this kingdom."

The archbishop agreed. Merlin conjured a huge marble stone in an open area in front of the cathedral. Under the marble was a stone and into the stone was driven a great sword, the most wonderful sword ever seen, extraordinarily bright and shining. The hilt was gold, carved and inlaid with beautiful precious stones that sparkled in the light. Near the sword was written in gold:

The Most Wonderful Sword

WHOSO PULLETH OUT THIS SWORD FROM THE STONE
THAT SAME IS RIGHT-WISE KING-BORN OF ENGLAND

People came to gaze on the sword and were
amazed at its beauty. The archbishop
announced that every man who wished to be
king must try to pull the sword from the stone;
whoever could do it would be the rightful king
of England.

When the order of the archbishop went out,
all the people of the kingdom stirred in wonder.

"Who shall be our king?" they asked. Some
thought it would be King Lot of Orkney or King
Urien of Gore, since these were the husbands of
Queen Igraine's daughters. Others thought it
would be King Leodegrance, father of the beautiful Guinevere. No one knew, but all were
eager to see who would be able to pull the sword
from the stone.

Then it seemed that the entire world was
traveling to London, for all the highways and
roads were jammed with kings and lords,

The Archbishop's Order

knights and ladies, esquires and pages. Every inn and castle was occupied with travelers. People pitched tents and pavilions along the wayside when no vacancies could be found.

When the archbishop saw the multitudes that had come to meet the challenge, he said to Merlin, "It would be amazing if from among all these great knights and kings, we could not find someone to rule the kingdom."

Merlin smiled and said, "Do not be surprised if among all these renowned kings and knights not one is found worthy. But also do not be surprised if among those who are completely unknown, one will prove himself to be rightful heir to the throne."

Who Will Remove the Sword?

Sir Ector and Sir Kay

CHAPTER 3

The Sword is Removed!

Sir Ector of Bonmaison was among those who came to London at this time. He was a noble knight and was held in great esteem by all who knew him. He had two sons. The eldest was Sir Kay, a young, courageous knight who was already well known in the courts of chivalry for his worthy deeds. The younger son, Arthur, had just turned eighteen. He served as Sir Kay's esquire-at-arms.

Sir Ector, being of such noble blood, welcomed the archbishop's order. He hoped Sir Kay would be the one to pull the sword from the stone. Sir Ector, Sir Kay and Arthur came to London and set up a pavilion displaying the emblem of their house, a black gryphon on a field of green. On the outskirts of London, numerous pavilions of noble houses filled the sky with a great many brightly colored pennants and banners.

The Archbishop of Canterbury, seeing so many lords and knights gathered for the grand contest of the sword in the stone, decided to hold a tournament of men-at-arms to see who was the most noble and accomplished knight.

When Sir Kay heard of this tournament, he asked his father's permission to compete. With his father's approval, Sir Kay, because of his noble blood, was allowed to enter. He chose his younger brother, Arthur, to be his esquire-at-arms. Arthur would carry his spear and pennant before him into the field of battle. He was extremely happy at the great honor he had been given.

The day of the tournament arrived. Over

An Esquire-At-Arms

twenty thousand lords and ladies came to see the proud young men do battle. The participating knights were divided into two groups, at the north and south end of the field. Sir Kay joined the north end, which had fewer knights, but included Sir Bedevere and others known for their great strength and courage.

The two groups met, one against the other, in the middle of the field. The sound of breaking lances was so extreme that many ladies screamed with fear as the air was filled with the splinters of shattered wood. In this famous battle many knights were defeated and others were trampled under the hoofs of the running horses. Some champions tried to raise themselves from the ground, but were too disabled. Attendants and esquires rushed to their leaders, replacing broken spears and destroyed armor.

During this battle, Sir Kay conducted himself with such credit that no knight did better. He fought knight after knight and defeated

A Fierce Battle

them. Half way through his battle he encountered Sir Balmorgineas, who called out to him, "Ho! Sir Knight of the black gryphon, turn this way and do battle with me!"

Sir Kay, full of spirited youth, turned with eagerness and fury to battle. He struck Sir Balmorgineas a fierce blow on the top of his helmet with his sword. Sir Kay's sword-blade broke from the force of the blow, and he was left with no weapon and at the complete mercy of Sir Balmorgineas. Three of his companions in arms, noticing his dilemma, protected him and brought him to the far end of the field to safety.

Young Arthur came running to him with a goblet of spiced wine. When he reached the barrier, Sir Kay drank quickly and called out, "Run as fast as you can to our pavilion and find me a new sword."

Arthur ran quickly but when he got to Sir Ector's pavilion he found no one. Everyone had gone to the tournament, and there were no swords to be found. Then Arthur remembered

Sir Kay's Sword Breaks!

the sword he had seen stuck in the stone near the cathedral. That sword would suit his brother's needs very well, he thought.

There was no one guarding the sword, so Arthur jumped on the rock and laid his hands on the hilt. In one quick movement he pulled the sword out of the stone with great smoothness and ease. He held the sword in his hand, and it was his!

He wrapped the sword in his cloak since it shone so brightly, and then he jumped down from the marble block and ran toward the tournament. When Sir Kay saw the sword he knew immediately what it was and stood in silence for a while, as if he had been turned to stone. Then, in a very strange voice he asked, "Arthur, where did you get this sword?"

"I will be honest, brother," answered Arthur, "I could not find a sword in our father's pavilion, so I thought of the sword I saw stuck in the stone near the cathedral. I went there and pulled at it and it came out with marvelous

Arthur Removes the Sword.

ease. I wrapped it and brought it to you."

Sir Kay's thoughts turned inward, and he said to himself: my brother Arthur is not more than a child, a very innocent child at that. He has no idea what he had done. Why shouldn't I say that I accomplished this and so get the glory it represents?

"Arthur," said Sir Kay, "Give the sword and the cloak to me, and tell no one what you have done. Go to our father and tell him to come to me immediately."

Arthur did as Sir Kay commanded him, not understanding why his brother seemed so disturbed. Young Arthur had no idea of the great deed he had done.

Arthur Brings the Sword to Sir Kay.

Arthur Runs to Sir Ector.

CHAPTER 4

Arthur's History

Arthur went to his father, as his brother had asked him to.

"Sire, my brother, Sir Kay, has sent me here and wishes you to come to him immediately," he told Sir Ector. "I think something extraordinary must have happened."

Sir Ector wondered what could cause Sir Kay to leave the battle and call on him at such a time. He immediately got up from the lists and followed Arthur back to the pavilion. There he saw Sir Kay's face was pale and that his eyes blinked nervously.

"My son, what is troubling you?" cried out Sir Ector.

"Sire, a wonderful thing has happened!" answered Sir Kay, and without another word unwrapped the cloak and revealed the sword. Sir Ector immediately knew the sword and where it had come from. He was amazed and didn't know what to do at first. Then he collected himself and asked, "What is this that my eyes see?"

To this Sir Kay replied, "I have that sword that stood thrust in the stone. Tell me, I demand, what this accomplishment may mean for me?"

But Sir Ector asked harshly, "How is it that you came by that sword?"

Sir Kay hesitated before he answered. "I broke my sword in battle and then I found this one to take its place."

Sir Ector was amazed and could not believe what his ears had heard. "If you pulled the sword from the anvil, then you are rightful heir

Sir Ector is Amazed.

and King of England. For the saying near the sword says this. But if you really were able to pull out the sword, then you can thrust it back into the stone it came from."

When he heard these words, Sir Kay was deeply worried. "How can one put the sword back? The stone is like solid iron. It would be impossible to thrust the sword back in."

"Not more impossible than to take out the sword in the first place," his father answered.

Sir Kay took comfort in knowing that his younger brother had already been able to pull the sword from the stone. "If young Arthur was able to do it, so can I," he said to himself.

So they wrapped the sword in the cloak and together Sir Ector, Sir Kay, and Arthur went back to the cathedral. Sir Kay looked at the stone, which had become smooth again, and said to himself, "Is there a man in life who could thrust a sword-blade into a solid stone like iron? Still I must try."

But it was impossible. He could not pene-

"No Man Can Perform this Feat!"

trate the iron. He tried and tried in vain. Finally, he called out to his father, "Sire, no man can perform this feat!"

But Sir Ector suspiciously answered, "How then was it possible for you to pull the sword out?"

"My father, may I speak?" young Arthur asked.

And Sir Ector said, "Speak, my son."

"I would like to try to push the sword into the stone, since I was the one who pulled it out." Arthur said. Arthur took the sword from his brother, Sir Kay, and jumped on the marble stone. He held the point of the sword against the stone and the sword penetrated as smoothly as it had been removed. He pulled the sword out again, and then once more put it back.

When Sir Ector saw what Arthur had done, he cried out in a loud voice, "Lord! Lord! I have witnessed a miracle." And when Arthur jumped down from the marble block Sir Ector knelt down before him.

Arthur Returns the Sword.

When Arthur saw his father kneel, he cried out, "My father! my father! why do you kneel before me?"

"I am not your natural father. It is now made clear that you are very exalted and the blood of kings flows in your veins."

All the while Sir Kay stood by like one mesmerized. Finally he said to himself, "What is this? Is my brother a king?"

Then Sir Ector spoke again. "The time has come, Arthur, for you to know the true circumstances of your birth which before now have been kept secret from you.

"Eighteen years ago, during the last year of the reign of Uther-Pendragon, a wise man known as Merlin came to me, carrying the King's signet ring. He ordered me by virtue of that ring to be in a certain place at a certain time near Uther-Pendragon's castle.

"He warned me to tell nobody of these orders, and I kept his instruction. I went to the place he told me, and two men came to me,

42

Merlin and Sir Ulfius

Merlin himself and Sir Ulfius. Merlin had in his arms a scarlet wrap of the finest texture. He opened the folds of the wrap and there lay a newborn child in swaddling clothes. You were that child.

"Merlin ordered me to take that child and raise him as if he were my own. He said the child was to be named Arthur, and no one in the world was to know from where I got him. From that day forward I have done as he instructed. Not until now have I ever really wondered who was your true father, though I believed you to be of royal blood. But now I believe you are the son of Uther-Pendragon himself!"

At these words Arthur cried out, "No! No! No!"

"Why are you sad, my king?" asked Sir Ector, kneeling once more to the young boy.

"Because I have lost my father," answered Arthur. "I would rather have my father back than be a king!"

While this was happening, there came to

"I Was to Raise Him As My Own."

the cathedral two men, very tall and of wonderfully noble and proud appearance. When they came closer, Sir Ector realized that they were Sir Ulfius and Merlin.

"What cheer?" asked Merlin.

"I have wonderful news," replied Sir Ector, "for here is the child you gave me eighteen years ago."

"I know," said Merlin. "In him lies the future of all England. He will become the greatest and most famous king that ever lived. Many knights of extraordinary strengths will gather round him. Men will tell of their marvelous deeds as long as the land will continue. Exalt, Sir Ector, for a great new age is here!"

In Him Lies the Future of England.

No King or Duke Succeeds.

CHAPTER 5

The New King

Finally, Christmas morning came. Thousands of people came to see the kings and dukes try to remove the sword from the stone. The archbishop sat upon his high throne, all his court of clerks and knights gathered around him.

Nineteen kings and sixteen dukes of royal lineage were to try to lift the sword from the stone. Those gathered were filled with excitement and anticipation.

The first to try the sword was King Lot of Orkney, son-in-law of Uther-Pendragon. He climbed the marble rock, saluted the archbishop and bent over the sword. He tried with all his might, but was unable to move the sword even slightly. Three times he attempted but each time he failed. Finally, he gave up.

King Urien, Uther-Pendragon's other son-in-law, was next to try. However, he did not succeed. Nor did King Fion of Scotland, or King Mark of Cornwall or King Leodegrance of Cameliard or King Pellinore. They tried with all their might. King nor duke was able to move the sword. Some were angered while others felt shame.

After all the kings and dukes had failed, the crowd began to whisper: "How is this? If all those kings and dukes of glorious rank have failed to achieve this, who then can do it?

The kings also began to talk among themselves. Then they approached the archbishop:

"Sir, here have all the kings and dukes of the realm tried before you to lift the sword from the stone and none have succeeded. Perhaps the

No King or Duke Could Remove the Sword.

enchanter Merlin has enchanted the sword only to bring shame and disgrace upon us. For who in the world could pull a sword from an iron stone? It is impossible. We ask you to select from your great wisdom one of us to become overlord."

"Have faith," the archbishop called out, "for I am sure Merlin will explain this to us all."

Merlin had told Arthur, Sir Kay and Sir Ector to keep hidden until he was ready for them. Now Merlin and Sir Ulfius walked into Sir Ector's pavilion and spoke:

"Rise, Arthur," Merlin called. "It is time for you to show the world the miracle you showed us."

Arthur did as Merlin asked and came from the pavilion dressed in scarlet embroidered robes.

They went to the cathedral and the great marble rock. The crowds let them pass as people asked, "Who are these with the enchanter Merlin and Sir Ulfius?" Merlin said nothing to anyone, but brought Arthur directly to where

Merlin and Sir Ulfius Enter the Pavilion.

the archbishop sat.

The archbishop rose and asked, "Merlin, who are these you bring with you and what do they intend to do?"

"Here is one to try to pull the sword from the stone," he answered and called Arthur forward.

"Merlin, by what right does this young man attempt to try the sword?" asked one of the angry kings.

"By the best right there is," shouted Merlin, "for he who stands before you is the true son of Uther-Pendragon!"

"But Uther-Pendragon had no children," cried out the archbishop.

"That is not true," answered Merlin and told the crowd of Arthur's secret birth.

"All that Merlin has said is true," exclaimed Sir Ector and Sir Ulfius. "Let the boy show you."

Then Arthur laid his hands on the sword, lifted it out of the stone and swung it around his head three times. He then placed it back in the stone. Now when the people who were assem-

Arthur Removes the Sword.

bled there saw this, they shouted so loud that it was as though the whole earth rocked and trembled.

While they shouted, Arthur took hold of the sword, lifted it from the stone and once more swung it around his head three times. Then he placed it back in the stone, picked it up yet again and repeated it for the third time.

All the kings and dukes were filled with great astonishment that a young man was able to perform what they had failed to do. Most were willing to acknowledge Arthur as the true king. Others, like King Pellinore, were angry in their hearts and vowed to fight the new king.

The archbishop proclaimed Arthur king of all England. The crowd gave another great shout. As Arthur left, the crowds followed after him, hoping to get near him or touch his clothes. Arthur was uplifted with great joy and happiness, so that his soul felt elevated and flew like a bird and soared through the sky.

Arthur Becomes King.

The Black Knight

CHAPTER 6

A Bitter Battle

A rumor had reached King Arthur in his court at Camelot of an evil knight in black armor who lived in a deep forest and attacked all who trespassed near his lonely castle. To the young king, conquering the black knight in battle would be a worthy deed. So in his armor, together with Merlin, he headed for the forest.

After some time they saw a stream of water that rushed through a dark and dismal valley. Over the water was a stone bridge and beyond the bridge a tall, dark, disagreeable castle. Over the bridge hung a black shield on which was written:—

WHOSO SMITETH THIS SHIELD
DOETH SO AT HIS PERIL.

On an apple tree beside it hung the shields of many knights who had attacked the black knight and had been defeated.

"This must definitely be a powerful knight who has defeated so many other knights. There must be a hundred shields hanging from that tree!" said King Arthur.

"May you be happy," replied Merlin, "if your own shield does not hang there before the day is over."

"That," said Arthur, "will be as God decides, since now I am more determined than ever to try my power against this knight." He seized his mace and hit the black shield a reverberating blow that echoed throughout the forest.

To this, the gates of the castle opened and out came a huge knight dressed in armor black

WHOSO SMITETH THIS SHIELD DOETH SO AT HIS PERIL

A Fearful Warning

as coal. He rode with much pride, as became a champion who had never been beaten in battle.

"Why did you dare to strike my shield? For your rudeness I shall take your shield and hang it upon that apple tree where you see the shields of others who dared to fight me," he called out.

"Know this, merciless knight," answered King Arthur, "I have come here to win back with my person all those shields that hang up on the tree. You will yield *your* shield to me!"

Each got ready his spear and shield. They shouted to their war-horses and drove toward each other. Those two noble horses rushed like lightning, dashing with violent speed. The two fierce riders crashed together like thunderbolts, and their spears burst into splinters.

Again, they tried with new spears, but once again the spears shattered and once again neither rider was able to knock down his enemy. Then they tried for the third time. King Arthur's spear burst into splinters but the

"You Will Yield Your Shield To Me!"

spear of the black knight stayed intact and struck the center of King Arthur's shield. The straps of the King's saddle burst from the violence of the blow and his horse was cast violently backward. King Arthur jumped off his horse with royal grace and landed on his feet. The hit he received was so painful that for a time he lost his senses and everything was blurred before his eyes.

When he had recovered, he cried out, "Come down, black knight, and fight me on foot and with your sword!"

"That I will not do," answered the black knight. "I have beaten you. You must surrender your shield to me."

King Arthur grabbed the bridle-rein of the black knight's horse and pulled it back so far that the black knight had to jump off his horse to keep from being knocked down.

Now each man drew his sword and charged together like two bulls in battle. They struck and dodged and struck again. The force of their

The Black Knight Demands the Shield.

strikes echoed throughout the forest. Complete chunks of armor were chopped from their bodies and each received numerous serious injuries. At last King Arthur struck such a blow with his sword that the black knight groaned and stumbled and ran around in circles. But the force of the blow had broken King Arthur's own sword so he was not able to complete his victory. The black knight recovered and taking his own sword into both hands struck King Arthur on his helmet with so powerful a strike that it cracked the helmet and seriously injured the king.

Seeing him so badly hurt, the black knight called for Arthur to surrender. Arthur would not give in but lifted himself up by his enemy's sword-belt. Then he circled the black knight with both arms, placed his knee behind the knight's thigh and cast him backward upon the ground. With that fall the black knight lost consciousness. Arthur immediately removed the knight's helmet and knew that it was none

Overthrown by His Horse

other than King Pellinore, his old rival.

"Ha! Pellinore, is it you? Now surrender to me, for you are at my mercy!" Arthur cried. He drew a small dagger and held it at his rival's neck.

By now Pellinore had recovered from his fall. Seeing how weak his enemy was from the head injury he had given him, he pushed the dagger away and hurled King Arthur to the ground. Pellinore picked up the dagger and made ready to kill his enemy.

"Stop, Pellinore," called out the voice of Merlin. "Hold your blasphemous hand! He who lies below you is none other than Arthur, king of all this kingdom!"

"If that is true, old man," shouted out Pellinore, "then you yourself have doomed him! For Arthur is my rival who has taken my land, my kingship, and my glory."

Merlin lifted his staff and hit Pellinore across the shoulders. Pellinore immediately fell down as if he were dead.

You Are At My Mercy!

Arthur observed his rival lying as though dead and cried out, "Merlin, what have you done? With your magic you have killed someone who has defeated me in fair battle!"

"Not so," said Merlin. "He is only asleep. You are much closer to death. Without my help, you will die soon."

With this said, Merlin carried the wounded Arthur across his horse and led him deep into the forest. He brought Arthur to a holy hermit skilled in treating injuries. He helped keep Arthur alive. But the young king was very weak and his recovery was questionable.

The next day, there came a great noise. It happened that the Lady Guinevere of Cameliard, along with her court, had decided to make a pilgrimage to see the holy hermit. In front of the hermitage, Guinevere saw King Arthur's pure white combat horse tied to a tree.

"Whose noble horse is that?" she asked Merlin, who stood nearby.

"It belongs to a knight who lies seriously

Lady Guinevere and Her Court

wounded inside," Merlin answered. "He is near death."

"Great heavens!" cried the Lady Guinevere, "may I see the injured knight?" So Merlin brought her into the hermit's abode. She did not know it was King Arthur, but thought she had never seen so noble a knight in her entire life. Arthur, almost unconscious, thought an angel from heaven had come down to visit him.

Guinevere had in her court an experienced doctor who took care of Arthur's wounds. When the lady and her court left, Arthur was almost completely healed.

This was the first time that Arthur ever saw that beautiful lady, Guinevere of Cameliard. From then on she was always on his mind and he swore that he would serve this lady as honorably as ever a good knight may serve his chosen lady.

Arthur Is Visited by Guinevere.

Arthur Wishes to Avenge His Wounds.

CHAPTER 7

The Forest of Adventure

Although Arthur had received terrible wounds from King Pellinore, he longed to try his enemy in battle again.

"If my sword had not broken," he told Merlin, "I may have defeated that knight. I will challenge him once again."

"But you have no sword and no spear, my lord," Merlin reminded him. "How can you intend to defeat him without any weapon?"

"Even if I had no better weapon than a wooden club, I would still take on King Pellinore once more," King Arthur said.

Seeing how determined King Arthur was in his purpose, Merlin told him the legend of Excaliber:

"Not far from here is the Forest of Adventure. Any knight that enters there will have an adventure ahead of him. In the middle of this forest of enchantment is a beautiful wide lake. In the center of that lake is a woman's arm, dressed in white samite. The hand holds a sword of such tremendous excellence and beauty that no eye has ever seen another like it. The name of this sword is Excaliber.

"Numerous knights have seen this sword and tried to get it. But not one has been able to reach it, and many have died trying. For when any man gets close to it, either he sinks into the lake or the arm disappears completely. Perhaps you can be the man who achieves the glory of capturing the sword."

"Lead me to this enchanted land," demanded the king. Merlin did so.

When they entered the enchanted wood-

The Enchanted Lake

lands, they saw a white doe with a golden collar. They followed her to an opening in the woods of soft smooth grass. A grove was set with a table of drinks, white bread, meats and wine. There stood at the entrance a page boy dressed all in green.

"Ho! King Arthur! Welcome!" he called out to them. "Come down and enjoy this meal."

Arthur hesitated, amazed that this page boy deep in the forest knew his name. But Merlin assured him that this was a good omen. They ate and replenished themselves. After, they came upon a meadow filled with the most beautiful flowers they had ever seen. This land was so radiant and so bright it seemed that it had been spun of gold. Rainbow-colored birds sung beautifully in the sky. Halfway through the meadow was a beautiful wide lake.

Merlin's prediction was there at the edge of the lake. In the middle of the lake was the fair and beautiful arm, covered in white samite. The hand held a sword of marvelous workmanship,

King Arthur is Welcomed.

the hilt crusted with precious jewels and the blade so radiant, it reflected like a shooting star.

King Arthur sat upon his war-horse. He was hypnotized by the sword. He wondered how he could reach it, since the lake was wide and deep. As he sat thinking, he suddenly saw an odd woman approaching through the tall flowers. He quickly got off his horse to meet her.

As he got closer to the woman he saw that she was very beautiful, with onyx black eyes as bright and glittering as two gems set in ivory. She was all in green and around her neck she wore a gorgeous necklace of opals and emeralds set in cunningly wrought gold. King Arthur knelt before her and said, "Lady, I see that you are no mortal woman, but are definitely a fairy. And I have entered an enchanted land."

The lady answered: "King Arthur, you are correct and I am indeed a fairy. My name is Nymue and I am leader of the Ladies of the Lake. And know you that what you see is not really a lake, but a meadow filled with flowers,

Excaliber

in the middle of which stands a white castle. To keep mortal eyes from seeing our home, my sisters and I have made an illusion of a lake through which no man can pass."

"Lady," said King Arthur, "I fear that in coming here I have trespassed on the solitude of your home."

"No, not true, King Arthur," said the Lady of the Lake, "for in reality you are quite welcome. I have great friendliness for you and the noble knights of your court. What brings you to this land?"

King Arthur told her of his combat, his need for a new sword, and how he wanted Excaliber. "That sword is not an easy thing to obtain," she answered. "No man may win Excaliber unless he is without fear and beyond disgrace."

"Lady," said King Arthur, "I do not lack in courage but there are things for which I do reproach myself. I will still attempt to win the sword. What is the best way?"

Then the Lady of the Lake whistled.

A Beautiful Fairy

Immediately a boat made of brass, quick as a swan, sped from the middle of the lake to the shore. The Lady of the Lake instructed King Arthur to enter the boat and immediately King Arthur felt the boat float quickly toward the sword. He reached forward and took the sword in his hand and the arm disappeared beneath the water. Then the king's heart leapt with joy, for Excaliber was a hundred times more beautiful than he had imagined.

The boat quickly carried him back and he gave the Lady of the Lake many thanks for all that she had done to help him. King Arthur and Merlin rode away, joyful at having achieved winning the most beautiful and famous sword in the entire world.

Arthur is Granted the Sword.

The King Strikes the Shield Again.

CHAPTER 8

To Battle!

It was midday when Arthur and Merlin reached the valley of the black knight. Everything looked the same as it did before; the dreary castle, the apple-tree covered with shields, the bridge where the black shield was hung.

"Now, Merlin," said King Arthur, "I do not condone your entering this fight. No magic shall determine right. It shall be between bold knights defending their valor."

The king rode forth on the bridge and once again struck the sable shield with all his strength. Immediately the gates of the castle opened and the black knight rode forth armed for the confrontation. As he came to the bridge-head, King Arthur spoke to him:

"Sir Pellinore, we now know one another well and each has his own opinions of the reasons for our fight. You feel that I have taken away your kingly estate and have driven you to the forest. I feel that you have set yourself here to do injury and to insult the knights in my kingdom. Let us fight, man to man, until one of us has defeated the other."

King Pellinore bowed his head in agreement and each combatant rode off a ways then sped forward to confront his rival. Once again their weapons burst into splinters but neither was able to knock down the other. Then each knight jumped off his horse and drew his sword. But now, having Excaliber to help him, King Arthur soon defeated his rival. He gave King Pellinore several wounds but received none himself. Finally, King Arthur delivered so bold a strike

The Enemies Confront One Another.

that King Pellinore felt his whole body go numb. He dropped his sword and shield and sank down on his knees. Then he called upon King Arthur to have mercy, saying, "Spare my life and I will submit to you."

King Arthur answered, "I will spare you and will go even further than that. For now that you have submitted yourself to me, I will return you to your power and your land. I bear you no ill will, Pellinore. But I can tolerate no rebels in this kingdom. As God judges me, I do rule singly in this realm. He who is against me is against my people, and he who is against my people is against me. As a symbol of your good faith, you will send me your two sons, Sir Aglaval and Sir Lamorack, to serve as knights in my court."

Then King Arthur carried King Pellinore back to his castle and made sure his injuries were taken care of. Peace and harmony were for some time brought to the kingdom.

Now as King Arthur and Merlin rode back to the court, Arthur was filled with joy and

"I Will Spare You."

pride over both his victory and his new sword. After some time Merlin asked the king:

"Arthur, which would you rather have, Excaliber or the sheath which holds it?"

Arthur answered, "Why, ten thousand times I would rather have Excaliber than its sheath."

"In this you are wrong, my lord," said Merlin, "It is true that Excaliber is so sharp that it can cut either a feather or an iron bar in two but its sheath is so magical that he who wears it will suffer no injuries in battle or lose a single drop of blood. As you saw in your last battle with King Pellinore you suffered no injuries whatsoever."

Then King Arthur looked angrily at Merlin, for all the happiness he had received from beating King Pellinore was now gone.

"Merlin, I must say that you have taken from me all the glory of that combat. There is no honor for any knight who defeats his enemy because of an enchantment. I have half a mind to take this magnificent sword back to the

"The Sheath is Magical."

magic lake and place it where it should be."

"My lord," said Merlin, "definitely you are correct in what you say. But remember that you are not a common knight, but a king. Your life belongs not to you but to your people. You have no right to endanger it but should do all that lies in your power to protect it. Keep the sword so that it may defend your life."

King Arthur pondered on this for a while and realized Merlin was right. However, he decided to use the sword only in serious combat. From then on, he fought no battles except with a lance and on horseback.

King Arthur truly cherished Excaliber and the sword was with him for his entire life. The sword became the most distinguished of any that ever were.

King Arthur Cherished Excaliber.

King Arthur Dines with His Court.

CHAPTER 9

Off to Cameliard

One day as King Arthur dined in Camelot in company of his knights, a herald-messenger arrived from the west-country. The messenger was from King Leodegrance of Cameliard, one of his first allies. He informed Arthur that their mutual enemy King Ryence of North Wales had demanded from King Leodegrance the return of land that bordered their countries. Ryence had also demanded that King Leodegrance hand over his daughter Lady Guinevere, to his nephew, Duke Mordaunt of North Umber. Now Duke Mordaunt, though a distinguished warrior was of malicious appearance and violent temper. However, King Leodegrance had no army to defend his kingdom so he called on Arthur for assistance.

When Arthur heard this news he became quite angry. He got up from the chair where he sat and went into an isolated room of the castle to be by himself. From the moment he had set his eyes on the Lady Guinevere in the hermit's hut, he thought her to be the fairest lady on earth. The thought of her marriage to the ugly and evil Duke Mordaunt drove him mad.

After sometime, he commanded Merlin, Sir Ulfius and Sir Kay to come to him. They all spoke for a long time. He bid Merlin to prepare himself for a trip with him. He told Sir Ulfius and Sir Kay to gather together a large army of the best knights and bring them to his castle at Tintagolon near the borders of North Wales and Cameliard.

They traveled the entire next day to Tintagolon without adventure or misadventure

He Pondered in an Isolated Room.

of any sort. Arthur was welcomed with great happiness, for wherever the king went, the people loved him dearly.

The next morning Arthur and Merlin walked in the woods. Arthur confessed to Merlin:

"Merlin, I do feel the Lady Guinevere is the fairest lady in the entire world. My heart is filled with great love for her. I think of her at all times, whether I am eating, drinking, walking or doing nothing at all. The thought of another man taking her for his wife drives me into a frenzy. I will not allow it!

"Now I know that you are gifted in the arts of magic that may alter a man's appearance so that even those who know him best can not recognize him. I wish you to disguise me so that I may go, unrecognizable to any man, to Cameliard so that I may see the Lady Guinevere every day. I wish to see her in such a way that she may not know my true identity. In this way I will also see the dangers that sur-

"I Will Not Allow Another to Marry Her."

round my good friend, King Leodegrance."

When he returned to the castle, Merlin came to the king and gave him a small cap. The cap was a magic one. When the king set it upon his head, in that moment he assumed the appearance of a plain and rustic lad from the countryside. The king ordered a jacket of rough fabric be brought to him and with this he covered his royal and knightly clothes and concealed the gold collar that he always wore around his neck. Then placing the cap upon his head, he assumed his disguise. Entirely unrecognizable, he left Tintagolon and headed on foot to the town of Cameliard, that was at the base of the castle.

He reached the castle itself by the end of the day. In the guise of a poor peasant from the countryside, no man in the world knew who he was. At the castle, he asked to speak to the head gardener. He asked him for work in that part of the garden near where he knew lived the Lady Guinevere. The gardener looked at him and

A Lad from the Countryside

saw a tall and well-built lad and hired him immediately.

This is how it came to be that King Arthur became a gardener's boy at Cameliard.

King Arthur Asks for Work.

King Arthur Admired Her from Afar.

CHAPTER 10

A Gardener's Boy?

King Arthur was happy to work in the garden since during this summer season the Lady Guinevere came every day for a stroll. For an entire week King Arthur enjoyed being a simple gardener without having the burden of kingship and being so close to the lady of his heart.

One day at dawn, when the weather was rather warm, one of Guinevere's attendants, the Lady Mellicene, looked out of the window that overlooked the rose garden beneath Guinevere's chamber. Below her she saw the figure of a noble knight bathing himself in the fountain. His reddish-gold hair was bright in the sun and around his neck he wore a gold collar of magnificent beauty.

Mellicene quickly ran down the turret stairs to find out how this noble knight had entered the garden. But King Arthur, hearing her coming, quickly put his magic cap on his head. When the young lady reached the fountain only the gardener's boy was there.

"Who are you?" demanded the lady. "Why are you sitting by the fountain and did you see the noble knight who was bathing here?"

"I am the gardener's lad," Arthur replied, "and there has been no one near the fountain today, only me."

Mellicene did not know what to think. She felt that the boy was deceiving her but also could not completely disbelieve him. She threatened to whip him if he deceived her and she reported what happened to her Lady Guinevere. Guinevere laughed and ridiculed

Mellicene Runs to See the Noble Knight.

her, telling her she had been dreaming when she saw the vision of the knight.

But then on another morning Mellicene saw the knight again. This time she woke her mistress and Guinevere also saw the noble knight. But this time he had taken off his golden collar as he washed. They hurried down the turret stairs to figure out what was happening.

Once again, King Arthur heard them coming and quickly put on his magic cap. The Lady Guinevere was amazed to see only the gardener's boy at the fountain and questioned him about the knight. Arthur told her that he was the only one who had been at the fountain that morning.

While rushing to put on his cap, King Arthur had forgotten about his golden collar. Suddenly Guinevere noticed it, shining in the sun.

"Do you mock me, boy?" she demanded of King Arthur. "How would a gardener's boy have a golden collar around his neck? I have a mind

"I'm the Only One at the Fountain."

to have you whipped. Take that collar and give it to the knight to whom it belongs. Tell him a true knight does not hide in a lady's garden."

That entire day as she sat over her embroidery, Guinevere wondered over the mystery and would attempt to solve it. Then she suddenly had an idea. She asked Mellicene to have the gardener's boy come inside and bring a basket of roses.

When King Arthur entered the lady's chamber, her attendants yelled at him for his rudeness.

"Remove your cap in the lady's presence," they cried.

"I cannot," answered Arthur.

"I command you take off your cap immediately!" Guinevere ordered.

"I cannot take it off because I have an ugly bruise on my head," said Arthur.

"Fine, then wear it," said Guinevere, but as he brought the roses to her, she suddenly reached for the cap and pulled it off his head.

Arthur Brings Flowers.

King Arthur was immediately transformed into his own self. He dropped the basket of roses which scattered all over the floor. Some of Guinevere's attendants cried in terror but Guinevere herself remained calm. She recognized him as the injured knight she had seen in the hermit's home.

Guinevere laughed mockingly and threw King Arthur's cap back at him.

"Take your cap," she said, "gardener's boy who has an ugly bruise on his head."

Arthur did not answer but with as much dignity as possible returned the cap to his head and was once more the gardener's boy. He turned and left, leaving the roses scattered on the floor.

Every time after, whenever Guinevere saw him, she would make a joke to him about his "ugly sore". However, she secretly told her attendants not to mention what had happened to anyone else in the court.

Arthur Transforms Into His Own Self.

Duke Mordaunt Threatening the Castle.

CHAPTER 11

The Knight in White

Trouble soon came to the Kingdom of Cameliard. King Ryence of North Wales and Duke Mordaunt persisted again, demanding the return of land and Guinevere's hand in marriage. Every day Duke Mordaunt paraded in front of the castle on horseback, challenging any knight of Cameliard to meet him. He was such a menacing knight, known for his skill and violence, that no one dared to take up his challenge. King Leodegrance listened to him gloat with shame and sadness.

All along, Arthur, working in the king's garden, was aware of everything that was happening. Finally he could not bear the insult to his lady any longer. He put aside his spade and through a back way traveled into the town. He took off his magic cap and found his way to the home of a wealthy merchant, Ralph of Cardiff. King Arthur showed the merchant his gold collar and his undergarments made of fine pure silk, embroidered with gold.

"Sir merchant," he said, "you have heard of the insults the Lady Guinevere and the people of Cameliard have received from the Duke Mordaunt. I am a noble knight who dares to take up the duke's challenge. However, I have no armor. I will leave these possessions in exchange for a worthy suit of armor. I give my knightly word that if I do not pay you for the armor after a time, you may have this golden collar and these fine clothes."

The merchant saw that Arthur was no ordinary knight errant and soon agreed. He found for Arthur the best armor he had for he also

Arthur Asks for a Suit of Armor.

wanted the defeat of the arrogant Duke Mordaunt.

The armor was skillfully wrought and inlaid with gold but the shield was pure white and had no crest on it. King Arthur mounted his horse and made his way through the stony streets of the town. Rumors began to circulate that a noble knight had arrived to take on Duke Mordaunt's challenge. King Arthur took an unpopulated route back to the queen's garden and asked to see the Lady Guinevere.

"My lady," he called out, "do I have your blessing to take up Duke Mordaunt's challenge in your name? Perhaps you will give me some token of your good wishes that I may take into battle with me."

"Sir Knight," replied Guinevere from her window, "I do wish I knew your identity. However, since no one else takes up this challenge, I grant you my blessing to fight for me. What token would you like me to provide for you?"

Arthur Asks Guinevere for Her Blessing.

King Arthur asked for Guinevere's necklace to wear on his arm. Guinevere took off the necklace and dropped it into King Arthur's waiting hand. He thanked her for her gift and with an uplifted and joyous heart rode out to do battle with Duke Mordaunt.

Rumor had spread throughout Cameliard that a knight was to go forth to meet the duke's challenge. Great crowds gathered on the walls. King Leodegrance and the Lady Guinevere came to where the castle wall overlooked the meadow patrolled by Duke Mordaunt.

The gates of the castle were suddenly lifted and the knight of the White Shield rode forward. The hoofs of his war-horse thundered and his armor blazed like lightning. A great cry of support went up from the people of Cameliard.

When Duke Mordaunt saw a knight dressed in white, he rode directly to him and spoke words of chivalrous greeting:

"Sir, I see that you carry no crest upon your shield, so I do not know who you are. Yet I

Guinevere Throws Down Her Necklace.

believe that only a knight of strong character dare challenge me."

"Sir Knight," answered King Arthur, "I am of character equal to your own. As for my courage, I believe I have fought as many noble battles as you."

"Say your prayers then," sneered Duke Mordaunt, "for I have beaten greater men than you."

To this insult King Arthur answered calmly, "That shall be decided by the will of Heaven, Sir Knight, and not by your own."

With that the two champions saluted each other and rode to their designated stations. Each clutched his spear and shield and made ready for the great confrontation. A deep silence fell upon the crowd as they waited for the battle to begin. Then, all of a sudden, each shouted to his war-horse and lurched forward. They met in the middle of the field with a sound like thunder. The spear of Duke Mordaunt shattered into splinters but King Arthur's spear did

They Saluted Each Other and Rode Out.

not. The duke was cast off his saddle and twirled about like a windmill, spinning in the air before he finally fell to the ground. Then he rolled over three times and lay absolutely still. His friends feared he was dead but he recovered after a few hours.

King Arthur was silent on his horse. He then quickly sped out of the forest. He was the anonymous conqueror who upheld the honor of his lady.

The Duke is Knocked from His Horse.

King Arthur in His Triumph

CHAPTER 12

The White Knight Once More

King Arthur, joyous in his triumph, rode forward to look for the knights of his court who had accompanied him to Tintagolon.

Meanwhile, Duke Mordaunt recovered from his injuries and plotted against King Leodegrance one again. "Surely the White Knight has left and no new challenger in Cameliard can defeat me," he thought.

He rode to the walls of the castle and called out his challenge to King Leodegrance:

"I propose a new offer to you. Tomorrow I ride out in the meadow with six of my most noble knights. If you find seven knights to take up our challenge and defeat us, I abandon my claim to the Lady Guinevere. But if you cannot, then not only will you hand over the lady for me to wed but you will give me three of the best castles that you own." Then his herald blew his trumpet and away rode the duke.

King Leodegrance felt great hopelessness since the White Knight had disappeared for two days and Leodegrance knew of no one else who could aid him. He went straight to his chamber and shut himself inside, for the marriage of his daughter to Duke Mordaunt was a thought he could not stand.

In the meanwhile, news reached Arthur and his knights of the duke's new challenge. Together with his nephew, Sir Gawaine and three other brave knights, Sir Geraint, Sir Ewaine and Sir Pelias, King Arthur hurried back toward Cameliard.

The day of the challenge came. The morning passed and part of the afternoon and still no

Duke Mordaunt Returns.

knights faced Duke Mordaunt and his companions. A cloud of dust suddenly appeared in the distance. Out of that dust emerged the five champions riding at great speed. The people of the town recognized Sir Gawaine, Sir Ewaine, Sir Geraint and Sir Pelias, for they were knights of great fame. Leading them was the White Knight, returning again in their time of need.

Duke Mordaunt arrogantly addressed the White Knight:

"Several days ago I lowered myself to fight you and you were lucky enough to knock me down. However, this is a more serious dispute. I will not fight you unless you identify yourself and tell me what your rank is. Beside, since we out number you by two, we cannot fairly fight you."

King Arthur did not answer but Sir Gawaine lifted his helmet and replied:

"Be cautioned, Duke Mordaunt, that I am at least of equal rank and status as you and the

Five Champions

White Knight is above me. You should be honored to compete against him. In regard to seven against five, the odds are equal when you compare our courage to yours."

At the sound of these words, Duke Mordaunt blushed and prepared for battle. A great silence fell over the crowd as the opponents turned to face each other. But in the first pass, King Arthur and his knights knocked down three knights, including Duke Mordaunt who was beaten by the White Knight. The strength of the White Knight's spear blow was so intense that Duke Mordaunt was instantly killed.

Arthur then turned to his knights and said: "My battle is done for the day. Now they are four and you are four. I will watch the bravery of my knights from afar."

With that, his knights returned to the lists and easily defeated the knights from North Umber who had lost all determination to fight after Duke Mordaunt's death. A magnificent

The White Knight is Victorious.

shout went up from the people of Cameliard and they opened the gates to welcome their heroes. But while King Arthur's knights entered the gates, the White Knight himself was nowhere to be found.

During the next days, King Leodegrance entertained his guests and thanked them for their help. The entire kingdom of Cameliard was happy and sure that peace had finally come. No one gave notice to the re-appearance of the gardener's boy who always wore a cap.

Then a daring herald from King Ryence came before King Leodegrance. The herald notified him that King Ryence was greatly angered by what had happened to Duke Mordaunt and re-issued his challenge for certain territories. If King Leodegrance did not comply then King Ryence would attack Cameliard with a large army.

Yet again King Leodegrance was filled with anxiety. Once again he wondered where he could find the White Knight who had already

A Herald from King Ryence

rescued his kingdom twice.

He called his daughter, Guinevere, because he had noticed that the White Knight seemed to have special consideration for her.

"My daughter," he said, "do you know how to call on the White Knight? We need his assistance since our enemy King Ryence is threatening at our doors."

"You would get more information from the gardener's boy about the White Knight than from me," answered Guinevere.

"Silly girl, do you joke when the kingdom is in danger?" shouted her father.

"No. Father, I do not joke. I have noticed that whenever the White Knight is before us, that boy is missing and whenever that boy is here, the White Knight is nowhere to be found."

The king immediately summoned the boy to be brought to him. When he entered, he was wearing his cap.

"Remove your cap when you are before me," demanded the king.

The King Summons His Daughter.

"I cannot remove my cap," King Arthur answered.

But then Lady Guinevere, who stood beside the chair of King Leodegrance spoke up. "I do implore you, for my sake, remove your cap."

When he heard this, he removed his cap and King Leodegrance immediately recognized him. He knelt before him, took Arthur's hands in his and said, "My lord, my lord, is it you who have performed these glorious deeds?"

Guinevere was amazed beyond measure. She had thought that Arthur was of noble blood but had not realized he was the king of the realm.

Arthur noticed that Guinevere had turned pale and spoke to her softly. "Lady, what bothers you?"

"I am afraid of your greatness," answered Guinevere.

"No, lady, instead it is I who am afraid of you," said Arthur. "For I love you so deeply that whether or not you have feelings for me is my

"It Is You Who Have Performed These Deeds?"

most important concern. Do you have feelings for me?"

"I do, my lord," said Guinevere softly.

"Do you have strong feelings for me?" asked Arthur.

"Yes, I do," smiled Guinevere.

Then Arthur lowered his head and kissed his lady before all who were there. At that moment they became engaged to be married.

Shortly afterwards King Arthur led his army to victory against King Ryence. He then looked forward to marrying Guinevere and bringing his beautiful queen to his court.

At That Moment They Became Engaged.

Preparations Were Made for the Wedding.

CHAPTER 13

The Royal Wedding

When autumn arrived, King Arthur at his court in Camelot made preparations for the arrival of his new bride. In anticipation of the wedding, the cobblestone streets were covered with flowers. All along the way that the royal couple would pass were hung tapestries of gold and crimson. Everywhere flags and pennants swayed in the warm gentle breezes.

King Arthur anxiously awaited the arrival of the Lady Guinevere and her court. At last the herald announced them. King Arthur and his court of knights brought King Leodegrance and

Lady Guinevere with great ceremony into Camelot and the royal castle while all around the townspeople cheered delightedly. When midday arrived, the entire court went with great splendor and royalty into the cathedral and there King Arthur and Lady Guinevere were married by the archbishop.

The bells of the city pealed joyfully and all the people outside the cathedral shouted their praise. For Arthur was greatly loved and admired by his people and they all were happy in his happiness. What followed was the most glorious wedding feast ever and all acclaimed the courtliness of Arthur and the beauty of Guinevere.

This was also the day that became renowned in chivalry because on this day the Round Table was founded. It was the flower and the major glory of Arthur's reign.

In the afternoon, Arthur and his court entered a fantastic pavilion that Merlin had built with magic. The walls were painted with

King Arthur and Lady Guinevere

beautiful images of angels and saints. The roof portrayed the sky and the stars overhead. In the middle of the sky was a likeness of the sun. The floor was a pavement of marble stones set in squares of black, white, blue, red and many other colors.

The Round Table which seated exactly fifty knights was in the center of the room. Before each seat was a gold dish filled with bread and a gold chalice filled with wine. When the king and his court entered, suddenly music played but there were no musicians anywhere.

Merlin led Arthur by the hand and took him to the center. "Here," he said, "behold the Round Table."

Merlin showed the king the numerous wonders of the Round Table. He pointed out a special high seat, wrought in precious woods. This was the royal seat designated for Arthur himself. As Merlin spoke, instantly on the back of the seat in gold letters appeared the words

KING ARTHUR

Behold the Round Table!

Opposite the royal seat, Merlin told Arthur, was the Seat Perilous. Only one man in all the world was worthy to sit there. If anyone unworthy tried to sit there, he would be punished with death. So it was called the Seat Perilous.

"Merlin," asked Arthur, "can we fill the seats of the Round Table with fifty knights?"

"No," answered Merlin, "for as of now there are but thirty-two knights noble enough to sit here." Merlin called off the name of each one and as he called them, their names in gold letters appeared on the backs of their seats.

"When the table is filled and there are fifty worthy knights," Merlin continued, "then your rule will start to fall into disarray. Because when any man has reached the peak of his glory, his work is done and God ruins him. So may a man break a chalice from which a wonderful wine has been drunk that a less desirable wine should never touch it. When your work is done, God will destroy the chalice of your life."

The Table Seats 50 Worthy Knights.

The king looked calmly at Merlin and said, "Wise man, your words are always filled with knowledge and wonder. Whatever fate befalls me, I will work for God's doing."

Thus was the Round Table founded with great splendor and festivities. The Archbishop of Canterbury blessed each and every seat and each chosen knight took his position at the table. All those who stood near the place, both knights and ladies, lifted up their voices in loud praise.

Then all the knights stood and each knight held up before him the cross of the hilt of his sword. Each knight repeated word for word the oath that King Arthur spoke. This was the covenant of their knighthood.

They would be merciful to the weak, show valor to the strong and be menacing to the evil. They pledged to protect the helpless who called upon them for assistance. They would regard all women sacred and they would protect each other in any way they were asked. They were to

The Covenant of Their Knighthood

show mercy to all men, be gentle in deed, sincere in friendship and faithful in love. Each knight swore to the covenant and then kissed the hilt of his sword. All present shouted once more in praise of their oaths.

Then all the knights of the Round Table seated themselves. They broke bread and poured wine, giving thanks to God for their food and drink and for eternal kinship.

So it was that King Arthur and Guinevere were married and the Round Table was founded.

They Broke Bread and Poured Wine.

An Enchantress

CHAPTER 14

Queen Morgana

King Arthur's stepsister, Queen Morgana le Fay, was a skillful enchantress. She was an expert on so much magic that with her powerful spells she could work her charm on all things. In earlier years she had been the student of Merlin. After him, she was the most powerful magician in the world. But unlike Merlin, she could not foretell the future.

Lately Queen Morgana had become quite upset with King Arthur for what she believed was an insult. Her son, Sir Baudemagus, had not been chosen to become a member of the

Round Table. Queen Morgana grew more and more angry at this rejection and felt she could not be happy in life unless she got revenge on Arthur.

But Queen Morgana was aware that she could never do her brother any harm as long as Merlin was there to guard him. She knew that in order to destroy the king she would have to destroy Merlin first.

At her court lived a young girl of magnificent and spellbinding beauty. She was of royal blood, being the daughter of the King of Northumberland. Her name was Vivien. Vivien was knowledgeable and crafty beyond her years. However, she was heartless and cold and vicious inside. Queen Morgana liked her and taught her all the magic and sorcery she knew. Still Vivien did not feel any love toward her teacher.

Vivien and Morgana sat together in a garden in Avalon, Queen Morgana's country, looking out over the beautiful ocean. Morgana

She Was Heartless, Cold and Vicious.

asked Vivien, "What do you wish for more than anything else in the world?"

"Lady, I would most want the knowledge you have far above anything else," answered Vivien.

Queen Morgana laughed and continued. "It is possible for you to become as knowledgeable as I am and even wiser too if you will follow my commands. For I know a way in which you may obtain that wisdom."

Vivien became curious and the queen continued. "Listen and I will tell. You must know Merlin, whom you have seen several times at the court of King Arthur. He is the master of all the wisdom that is possible for anyone to possess in this world. Everything that I know of sorcery, Merlin has taught me. And he knows many things that he has not shown me. Merlin taught me when I was young because I was beautiful and caught his eye. For Merlin loves female beauty more than anything in this world and so he taught me magic and was most

"Merlin Has Taught Me All I Know."

tolerant with me.

"But Merlin has a great ability which belongs to him alone and which he cannot impart to anyone else, since it is instinct with him. That is the gift of divination and fore-telling.

"While he has the ability to foresee the fate of others, he is unable to do so for himself. He confessed this to me several times. Vivien, you are even more beautiful than I was at your age and besides I will give you a certain enchant-ment that will make you irresistible to Merlin. He will love you so much that he will confide more wisdom to you than he did to me.

"Keep in mind that as your beauty fades, he may regret relating this knowledge to you and may cast a spell upon you to prohibit you from using your powers. Because the world cannot hold two people who are so magically gifted."

Vivien listened with a great deal of atten-tion and when Queen Morgana had finished, she said, "My lady, everything that you tell me

"Merlin Will Tell You Everything."

is wonderful and I want to learn all Merlin's secrets. If you will assist me in this endeavor, I will be forever indebted to you. Do not worry about the danger involved because I will use the wisdom Merlin gives me to enchant him and he will never again be able to harm me or anyone else. I will use my cleverness against his knowledge, my beauty against his skill and I believe I will win this game."

Queen Morgana laughed so hard she could not stop. "Certainly, Vivien, you are skillful beyond your years. No one would imagine so young a girl could bring about the downfall of the world's craftiest magician!"

With that, she put a thin whistle to her lips and blew. Servants came in carrying a casket of alabaster filled with precious jewels. Morgana selected two rings, one with a clear white stone, the other with a bright red one.

"Vivien," she said, "look at these two rings. They are each enchanted with a spell of incredible power. If you wear the ring with the white

Enchanted Jewels

stone, whoever wears the ring with the red stone will love you with an incredible passion, so strong that he will do whatever is your bidding. Take these rings to King Arthur's court and use your skill to bring down Merlin."

Vivien was grateful to Queen Morgana for all she had shared with her. She thanked her and left with the two enchanted rings.

Vivien Was Grateful.

Vivien Brings the Ring.

CHAPTER 15

The Feast of Pentecost

Every Pentecost, King Arthur took great pleasure in holding a great celebration. His court gathered around him for mirth, good cheer and entertainment. As all the nobles sat at the feast, suddenly into the hall came a beautiful young lady and a monstrous dwarf. The lady was dressed in scarlet satin, her hair was auburn and her eyes glistened like onyx. The dwarf was also dressed in red and carried in his hands a cushion of red silk with tassels of gold. On the cushion was a ring of magnificent beauty set with a ruby.

King Arthur thought he recognized the young lady and asked her who she was.

"I am the daughter of the King of Northumberland. My name is Vivien," she answered.

King Arthur asked her what she had on the pillow and why she had brought it to the celebration.

"Lord, I have very good entertainment for Pentecost. Here is a ring that only he who is the most knowledgeable and worthy of all men may wear."

"Let me see this ring," said King Arthur.

Vivien took the ring from the cushion and brought it to King Arthur. The king took the ring into his own hands and asked to try it on. However, when he tried to put the ring on his finger, it shrank in size so that it could not pass beyond the first joint.

"It appears that I am not worthy to wear this ring," he laughed.

"My lord," asked Vivien, "Will you allow me

King Arthur Tries on the Ring.

to have others in your court try?"

King Arthur agreed. Several members of the court tried on the ring but it fit no one. Then Vivien came to the place where Merlin sat. She kneeled before him and offered him the ring. Since Merlin could not foresee his future, he saw no harm directed at him. "Child, what is this silly thing?"

"Sir," answered Vivien, "I beg you to try this ring upon your finger."

Merlin examined her closely and was charmed by her great beauty. He said in a more gentle tone to her, "Why should I take the ring?"

"Because I believe you are the most wise and worthy man in this realm and the ring belongs to you," Vivien answered.

Merlin smiled and took the ring and placed it upon his finger. It was a perfect fit. Vivien cried out, "Look, the ring fits!"

Merlin was pleased at first. But when he tried to remove it, he could not because the ring had attached itself to his finger as if it were of

Vivien Gives Merlin the Ring.

his flesh and bones. Merlin became upset about the magic in the ring.

"Lady," he asked, "from where did you get this ring?"

"Sir," answered Vivien, "you can see everything. Why do you not know that this ring was sent here by Morgana le Fay?"

Merlin grew more concerned and said, "I hope there is no malice in this ring."

Vivien smiled at him and answered, "What malice could there be in it?"

By this time the enchantment in the ring had started to work on Merlin's spirit. He became more and more attracted to Vivien's beauty. Soon his infatuation was so great it was as if his very heart was pierced.

Vivien saw the effect of the ring and laughed and turned away. Many noticed the strange manner in which Merlin fancied her but attributed it only to Vivien's loveliness.

Shortly after, the enchantment of the ring grew so intense that Merlin could not release

Merlin Cannot Remove the Ring!

himself from Vivien's sorcery. He followed wherever she went. And all the court laughed and joked at the old man pursuing the young girl. Vivien despised Merlin with all her heart and he annoyed her with his admiration. But she pretended to have a great affection for him.

Now one day as she sat in the garden, Merlin followed her. She stood quickly to escape him but Merlin hurried and caught up to her.

"My lady," he asked, "is it true that you despise me?"

"Sir, I do not," answered Vivien.

But Merlin did not believe her.

"What can I do to make you love me?" he asked.

Quickly Vivien answered, "If you would relate to me your great wisdom and skill, I believe I could love you."

Merlin looked intensely at Vivien and realized she was not as innocent as she looked. But still his love for her was so great that he agreed to teach her all his magic.

"What Can I Do To Make You Love Me?"

A while later, Vivien asked King Arthur for permission to go and visit her father in Northumberland. King Arthur agreed and Merlin left with her. However, they did not go to Northumberland. Instead they left for a secluded place where Merlin agreed he would teach her all the sorcery he knew.

They Left for a Secluded Place.

Merlin Conjures a Castle.

CHAPTER 16

Merlin's End

Merlin and Vivien, along with their attendants, headed deep into the woods. It was a secluded and deserted place and Merlin's followers began to panic.

"The sorcerer has brought us here but how will he provide shelter when the weather changes?"

Merlin learned of their worries and promised them they would soon find a good resting place. Then he told them to step back while he performed a spell. Merlin recited a powerful incantation and before their very eyes they saw images flash before them that rose high into the air. Then a cloud of red dust covered their eyes. When the dust cleared, they saw a magnificent castle which shimmered in the moonlight.

When Vivien saw what Merlin had done, she kneeled before him, took his hand in hers and kissed it.

"Master," she said, "will you show me how this was done?"

"I will teach you how to do this and much more besides. I will teach you how to manipulate shapes. I will teach you enchantments and charms that no man has ever heard before."

"You are the most wonderful man in the world," Vivien cried out.

"You don't hate me anymore?" asked Merlin.

"No, master," she answered.

But she deceived him because in her heart she was malicious and the heart of Merlin was good. That which is evil will always hate that which is good. While Vivien spoke lovingly to

"Will You Teach Me These Things?"

Merlin, inside she despised and feared him. She knew that without the magic ring, he would know that she was truly evil. As soon as Merlin has taught me all he knows, the world will be too small for both of us, she thought, and I will destroy him.

Merlin and Vivien lived together in that place for over a year. He taught her all of the magic he was capable of. When he had taught her everything , he said to her, "Vivien, I have now taught you so much that I believe there is no one in all of the world who knows more magic than you do."

Vivien was thrilled at these words. She told herself, "Now Merlin, if I am lucky enough to trap you in my spells, you will never see the world again."

The following day Vivien called for a celebration to be prepared for herself and Merlin. Using the knowledge she had learned from Merlin, she prepared a very powerful sleeping potion which she poured into Merlin's chalice.

Vivien Makes a Poisonous Drink.

When the celebration had come to an end, Vivien went to Merlin and said:

"Take this chalice and drink the wine I have poured. The wine is noble and so are you." She pretended to put her lips to the chalice and kiss it but she did not really drink from it. Merlin suspected no malice and drank the wine happily.

Shortly, the fumes of the sleeping potion began to effect him. Merlin realized he had been fooled.

"Help! Help!" he cried out in pain. "I have been betrayed!"

He tried to get up but fell backwards.

Vivien sat with her chin upon her hands and observed him closely, smiling maliciously at him. When Merlin fell into a deep sleep, Vivien cast a powerful spell around him that bound him in a web of enchantment. Merlin was like an insect caught in a silver spider's web.

The following morning when Merlin woke from sleep, he saw Vivien looking at him but he

Merlin Fell Backwards!

could not move.

"Behold, Merlin, you are completely in my power. You cannot move an inch without my will. And now I will leave you to go into the world. All your power and magic will now be mine."

Vivien struck her hands together and called her attendants. She presented Merlin before them and made them pull at his beard and pinch his arms and hands but Merlin was helpless. They all laughed at Merlin and mocked him. Then Vivien used her sorcery to make a great coffin of stones. She had Merlin placed on the coffin and then covered it with a huge stone slab.

She then used her power to make the castle disappear. She created a terrible mist that no one could be able to see through. This was the end of Merlin.

Vivien Cast a Spell Over Merlin.

Sir Launcelot

CHAPTER 17

Turmoil in the Kingdom

Sir Launcelot was the greatest of all the knights of the Round Table. He was known for his valor, his courage and his handsome appearance. No knight accomplished more difficult deeds, no knight saved more ladies and no knight defended the weak as well as did Sir Launcelot. Because of his great character and great goodness, King Arthur loved and trusted him the most of all his knights.

Sir Launcelot was also a good friend of Queen Guinevere. As soon as he arrived at Camelot, he pledged his loyalty to her and all the actions he performed were for her regard. The queen admired Sir Launcelot and loved to listen to him tell stories and sing and dance. He would join her on trips and often visit her private room in the castle.

Now terrible rumors began to spread that the queen and Sir Launcelot were more than friends. And after a time, the rumors began to reach the ears of the king. Initially he paid no attention. But as the rumors continued, he grew cold toward his wife and his trust in Sir Launcelot weakened.

These rumors were spread by members of the court who were jealous of Sir Launcelot. Among those was Sir Modred, King Arthur's nephew, who wished to gain the throne for himself.

One night, Sir Modred called a page of the queen's court and said, "Go to Sir Launcelot and tell him the queen wishes to speak to him." The page delivered his message and Sir Launcelot, suspecting no wrong, went to the queen's apart-

A Page and Sir Modred

ment.

Guinevere was not expecting him and Launcelot became immediately suspicious for he knew he had enemies at the court. Meanwhile, Sir Modred waited at the entrance to the queen's apartment until he saw Sir Launcelot enter. The he ran to his brother, Sir Agravaine, and told him that Sir Launcelot was in the queen's private chamber betraying the king. Sir Agravaine called together eleven knights and headed to the queen's apartment to arrest Sir Launcelot.

But the lady attendants of the queen saw the knights headed toward her chamber and warned Guinevere and Launcelot of the plot against them. They locked the doors to protect themselves.

Sir Agravaine knocked and cried aloud in a thunderous voice:

"You betraying knight! What have you come to do here behind the queen's locked doors? Come out to us, your fellows of the Round Table

At the Queen's Chamber

and explain."

Sir Launcelot looked around the queen's chamber for a suit of armor to protect himself but found none.

"Lady, I must go out and fight them without armor," he told Guinevere. "But if I am to die, go to my kin and ask asylum. You will no longer receive justice at this court. Camelot, once the fairest place on earth, is now poisoned with treachery and betrayal."

By then, Sir Agravaine, Sir Modred and their allies had a battering ram and were trying to break through the doors. But Sir Launcelot opened the door just a little, enough to allow one knight, Sir Colgrance of Gore, to enter. The knight, seeing Sir Launcelot unarmed, struck a quick blow with his sword. But Launcelot missed the blow. With his own sword he struck down Sir Colgrance and quickly closed the door.

"My queen," he called out, "help me into this armor. Then I can make my escape."

Breaking Through the Door

Sir Launcelot, now in armor, opened the door and took on the group of knights who had come to attack him.

Immediately, he killed Sir Agravaine and in the battle killed seven other knights including Sir Florence and Sir Lovel, the young sons of Sir Gawaine. He wounded Sir Modred, who made his escape.

Sir Launcelot turned to Queen Guinevere and cried aloud:

"My lady, I must leave here forever, since tonight I have killed the nephew of the king and two of the sons of my dear friend, Sir Gawaine. However, I will not abandon you. They will come to try you for treason tomorrow. I leave now to gather knights loyal to me and we will come to save you."

The queen fell crying on her bed. "The end of our beautiful kingdom is near," she sobbed. "Oh, Camelot!"

Sir Launcelot Kills Eight Knights.

The King Gets Word.

CHAPTER 18

Escape!

Sir Modred had his wound tended to and headed for the inn where he knew King Arthur was staying. When King Arthur saw his nephew with an injury he inquired about what had happened. Modred explained that Sir Launcelot had been caught in the queen's private chamber and when confronted had killed, among others, the king's nephew, Sir Agravaine, and the two young sons of Sir Gawaine before he had fled.

The king groaned aloud and declared that next day the queen would be tried for treason.

Then he went to a private place to mourn.

"All has happened as Merlin predicted," he said to himself. "All my kingdom falls back into savagery and the end is near."

Then he commanded the queen be brought to trial in a plain robe and barefoot. "For I will not believe her innocence until it is proved so," he sighed.

When the queen heard that she was to be dressed as a common criminal, she cried bitterly. "My lord, the king, has already judged me in his heart," she cried, "so that my trial will mean my death!"

Rumor of the trial reached Sir Launcelot. He had brought together the knights of the Round Table loyal to him, including Sir Bors and Sir Lionel.

As the queen was led barefoot to her trial, Sir Launcelot rushed to her rescue. For the first time, knights of the Round Table battled each other in deadly combat. Sir Launcelot, in fierce battle, struck and killed Sir Gareth and Sir

"The Trial Will Mean My Death."

Geharis who had been two of his dearest comrades-in-arms. Finally, Sir Launcelot reached the queen. He unbound her and pulled her on to the saddle of his own horse.

"Let us take flight, while there is still time!" he called to his men. Together with the queen and the knights still faithful to him, Sir Launcelot fled to his castle, Joyous Gard, where he offered the queen peace and asylum.

Meanwhile, in the battle, twenty-seven knights of the king were killed and sixteen of Sir Launcelot's party. Among them was King Arthur's old friend, Sir Kay. As Arthur looked down at the body of his friend, he saw another sign that the kingdom was nearing its end.

The bold actions of Sir Launcelot could be called the beginning of the end of King Arthur's reign. Sir Launcelot had come between the law and the queen because he felt obligated by his honor to love and protect her.

King Arthur was also obligated to regain his queen and punish her as a lawbreaker. That

They Escaped to Joyous Gard.

she had gone off with Sir Launcelot was an act the king could never allow or forgive.

When the news of the battle reached King Arthur, he was filled with anger and grief.

"The happiness of the Round Table is gone to sadness," he said, "and it will never be the same again." Merlin's prophecy surely would be fulfilled.

By now Sir Gawaine had sworn relentless hatred of Sir Launcelot and encouraged King Arthur to attack Joyous Gard. Arthur hesitated, not from fear, but because he didn't want to attack those of his own knights of the Round Table who had sided with Sir Launcelot. Reluctantly he called on all his remaining knights and ordered the attack.

Sir Launcelot and his brother Sir Ector stood at the wall of Joyous Gard and watched the great army of King Arthur as it headed towards them.

"Would it not be better to compromise with the king and return his queen to him?" Sir

The Battle Begins!

Ector asked his brother.

"Never," replied Sir Launcelot, "unless the king will give me his word that no harm will come to her, I will not give her up. That would bring great dishonor to us."

So it was that the war continued.

Sir Ector Suggests a Compromise.

A Deadly Battle

CHAPTER 19

Joyous Gard is Attacked

King Arthur's army made attack after attack on the castle of Joyous Gard. They made holes in the walls. But these gaps were repaired during the night. Each side lost many men and both armies suffered terribly.

The advisors to Sir Launcelot decided it was best to make a break through the king's army and reach the sea so that they could journey to France and safety. Sir Launcelot tried one last time to make peace between himself and Arthur.

That afternoon he appeared on the battlements of his castle and asked to speak to King Arthur. Arthur's army thought that perhaps Sir Launcelot was going to surrender. They ran to the king. King Arthur hurried to ask Launcelot if he would indeed surrender.

"I would speak to you of other things," said Sir Launcelot. "Why are you attacking this castle? Inside are many brave knights of the Round Table. Is it to your honor to kill these worthy, honorable knights?"

"You forget, sir," called King Arthur, "that you have unlawfully captured my queen. Surrender her to me and we can talk further."

"Your queen is held in high honor here, safe from harm. Promise her safety to me and I will surrender her to you."

"Am I to make a bargain for the return of my wife?" asked Arthur disdainfully.

Then Sir Gawaine spoke up. "Sir, have you forgotten you killed two of my brothers and two of my sons? There will never be peace between us!"

ments of his castle and asked to speak to King Arthur. Arthur's army thought that perhaps Sir Launcelot was going to surrender. They ran to the king. King Arthur hurried to ask Launcelot if he would indeed surrender.

"I would speak to you of other things," said Sir Launcelot. "Why are you attacking this castle? Inside are many brave knights of the Round Table. Is it to your honor to kill these worthy, honorable knights?"

"You forget, sir," called King Arthur, "that you have unlawfully captured my queen. Surrender her to me and we can talk further."

"Your queen is held in high honor here, safe from harm. Promise her safety to me and I will surrender her to you."

"Am I to make a bargain for the return of my wife?" asked Arthur disdainfully.

Then Sir Gawaine spoke up. "Sir, have you gotten you killed two of my brothers and two my sons? There will never be peace between

212

Sir Ector Suggests a Compromise.

A Deadly Battle

CHAPTER 19

Joyous Gard is Attacked

King Arthur's army made attack
attack on the castle of Joyous Gard. They
holes in the walls. But these gaps were r
during the night. Each side lost many r
both armies suffered terribly.

The advisors to Sir Launcelot deci
best to make a break through the k
and reach the sea so that they coul
France and safety. Sir Launcelot t
time to make peace between
Arthur.

That afternoon he appeared

f
s

m

for
of
us!"

Sir Launcelot Talks to King Arthur.

"Then God pity us for our un-Christian hatred," called Sir Launcelot as he left.

It was decided in the castle to prepare for battle and take flight. All of a sudden, the walls to the castle were thrown open and Launcelot and his men burst forth in their daring attempt to break through the king's army.

Initially the charge seemed successful but then Launcelot saw they were lost and they would be quickly cut off.

"Retreat! retreat!" he called. Together he and the queen barely made it back into the castle. Many died in the attempt, including Launcelot's dear friend, Sir Lionel. The cost of the war grew deeper and deeper.

The Bishop of Rochester came to the camp of King Arthur to try to make peace between the fighting armies.

"Lord," he asked, "let this combat between you and Sir Launcelot end. Let there be peace once more in the land. For friend fights against friend and brother fights against brother. What

They Attempted to Escape.

good or honor can come from such a war?"

"I did not start this war," answered the king. "It was Sir Launcelot's fault. He and his fellows took my queen. Let them deliver the queen and there will be peace."

"They will not deliver the queen unless you declare upon your honor that no harm shall come to her."

Then the king sat with his fist on his forehead and thought about what the bishop had said.

Finally, in a broken voice he said to the bishop, "Let the queen be delivered to me at Camelot and I promise no harm shall be done to threaten or deprive her of her life."

"Let me have that in writing," said the bishop. King Arthur called for a scribe and wrote those words and handed them to the bishop who hurried off to Joyous Gard.

The queen read the agreement and was satisfied on her own behalf but worried about all the knights that had remained loyal to her.

Arthur Thought Over the Bishop's Words.

They had not been mentioned in the document.

The bishop returned to Arthur with those concerns.

"What other conditions do they want from me? Why should I promise no harm to those who have acted treasonably against me?" But then Sir Gawaine whispered something to Arthur and the king turned to the bishop and said:

"Very well, take my word to these knights that I will do no harm to them as long as they are within the kingdom of England."

The Bishop relayed the news to Sir Launcelot.

"Let the king return to Camelot and within three days time I will return the queen to him."

So ended a sad and vicious war in which many brave knights lost their lives and the fellowship of the Round Table was forever destroyed.

King Arthur Agrees to the Conditions.

The Queen is Brought Before the King.

CHAPTER 20

Challenge to Sir Launcelot

The king returned to Camelot and on the third day the queen was brought to him. Sir Launcelot and Queen Guinevere wore olive branches, symbols of peace, on their heads and approached the throne and knelt.

"King Arthur," said Sir Launcelot, "I return to you your queen. For thirteen weeks she has lived in my castle with the highest honor. I return her to you as pure as when you first saw her in Cameliard."

King Arthur frowned. For a while he said nothing and then finally spoke:

"Sir, you were once my friend and the best beloved of all my knights. But that has now changed and will never be the same. You stole my queen by force for several months. Through your actions, many brave knights have died. Now you come before me and plead with me to accept my queen with love and affection. That which has been undone must remain undone. The seat beside my throne will remain forever empty.

"Never again shall Queen Guinevere or any queen sit here. Guinevere I reject completely. I have promised no harm will come to her and herewith I give her over to the church where she shall remain a nun until the end of her days.

"As for you and your knights, I promised no harm would come to you on English soil. But from this moment forth you are hereby banished from this land forever and cannot return unless you wish to die. And all your lands and properties shall be forfeit to the king."

"You Are Banished!"

Thus the queen was taken away to an abbey, there to spend the rest of her days, while Sir Launcelot and his friends left for France, where they lived in great sorrow.

But still, even after they had left, anger burned inside Sir Gawaine, for he had sworn undying hatred of Sir Launcelot. Eventually, he convinced King Arthur to attack Sir Launcelot in France. Arthur had agreed, Gawaine argued, not to attack Sir Launcelot in England. But he had the right to attack him in France. Sir Gawaine convinced the king and Arthur gathered an army and set forth for France. He left his nephew, Sir Modred, in charge in England.

King Arthur and his army besieged Sir Launcelot in his castle at Chillion. As before, many brave knights died in the struggle. But the walls of the castle held. Then Sir Gawaine decided that he wanted to challenge Sir Launcelot directly.

The next morning he paraded in front of the castle calling Sir Launcelot to fight. But Sir

The Queen Went to an Abbey.

Launcelot, who still had a great love for his old friend, refused. But each and every morning Sir Gawaine's provoking grew worse and on the fourth morning Sir Launcelot came out ready to fight.

Never before had there been seen such a battle. Sir Gawaine fought with the strength of ten men but still the superior skill of Sir Launcelot defeated him. And when Sir Gawaine's shield lowered, Sir Launcelot struck him a blow that pierced his armor and injured him fatally. When Launcelot asked Gawaine for forgiveness, Gawaine refused, saying he would die his enemy.

They carried Sir Gawaine's wounded body to King Arthur's tent. There Arthur saw his dying nephew and groaned aloud. But Sir Gawaine suddenly spoke to him in a clear voice:

"My lord, now that I am near death, it is as if a blindfold has been removed and I can see clearly. Sir Launcelot was never your true rival. It was Sir Modred who plotted against you

"I Will Die Your Enemy."

both. Even now in England he seizes your throne and plans to kill you when you return." With these words, Sir Gawaine closed his eyes and died.

King Arthur cried at the loss of his noble kinsman and promised to seek revenge against Sir Modred.

Sir Gawaine Dies.

On the Far Side, an Injured Knight

CHAPTER 21

The End of the Reign

King Arthur made peace with Sir Launcelot and led his army back to England. However, waiting for him at the cliffs of Dover was Sir Modred and an army loyal to him. Yet Sir Modred could not keep King Arthur's army from landing. They fought a terrible battle by the shore, brother against brother, friend against friend, until the ocean was red with blood.

But finally the army of King Arthur was victorious, and the army of Sir Modred broke and ran. Late that night, the king, accompanied by Sir Bedevere looked over the battlefield. On the far side he saw an injured knight walking in the mist.

"Sir Bedevere," he cried out, "isn't that my nephew, the traitor Sir Modred? Give me your spear so I may end him forever!"

"But sire," said Sir Bedevere, "that is a desperate man without friends or family. Do not challenge him, for he can turn on you like an injured animal in its rage."

But King Arthur said, "What does my life matter now that I have lost my wife, the love of my youth and all those knights, the chief glory and pride of my reign? What have I to live for besides an empty throne?"

With these words he grabbed Sir Bedevere's spear and rode off to challenge his enemy. Sir Modred drew his sword and it flashed like lightning in the darkness. He came forward to meet King Arthur, whirling his sword on high. But the king drove the point of his spear into Sir Modred with such force that the spear came out

Revenge on Sir Modred

through his back. Sir Modred knew he had received his death wound. But with a strength almost inhuman, triggered by revenge, he pushed himself up the length of the spear and struck the king such a fierce blow that his sword cut through King Arthur's helmet.

The king reeled on his saddle and Sir Bedevere quickly caught him and brought him to his tent. But when his helmet was removed, Arthur knew he had received his final wound. In a calm voice he asked Sir Bedevere to take his sword, Excaliber, and throw it deep into the water of a nearby lake.

Sir Bedevere ran to follow his king's last command. But when he reached the lake shore and looked at Excaliber, he reconsidered. "It seems a waste to throw this beautiful sword into the water. I will keep it for myself and tell the king I did what he wanted," Sir Bedevere decided.

When he returned, King Arthur asked him what happened to the sword.

King Arthur Receives His Final Wound.

"I saw nothing but the waves beating on the shore," said Sir Bedevere.

"What? Do you betray me while I'm dying? Go back again and throw the sword into the lake!"

Sir Bedevere begged the king's forgiveness and once again returned to the lake shore. But yet again he could not make himself throw the sword into the lake.

When he returned, King Arthur again asked him what happened to Excaliber.

"I saw the moon shining high in the sky and nothing else," answered Sir Bedevere.

"Still do you deny my last wishes," cried out Arthur.

"Forgive me," begged Sir Bedevere and for the third time he took the sword to the lake. This time he threw Excaliber in as far as he could. To his surprise, an arm covered in white samite reached up from the center of the lake. Its hand grabbed the sword and pulled it smoothly into the water. Excaliber was gone.

"Return the Sword!"

He ran back to tell King Arthur what had happened.

"You have done well, Sir Bedevere," said Arthur. "Now take me to the shore, for there is a boat there waiting for me."

Sir Bedevere did as his king asked. There was a brass boat waiting. In it was the Lady of the Lake, Nymue, who had come for Arthur.

When Arthur was placed in the boat, Sir Bedevere cried:

"My king, you are dying and I will have no one."

King Arthur opened his eyes and said:

"Know that I will not die at this place. For the Lady of the Lake has come to take me to the valley of Avalon where I will yet live for a long time. The lady will come when I will return to England. And with my return will come peace, there will be no more war. Take back this news and goodbye."

So it was that the magnificent King Arthur was gone.

"I Will Bring Peace."